AF435820

MATILDA MARTEL

SUMMARY

She's a Park Avenue princess---untouchable and far beyond his reach. He's the son of a mafia don, arranged to marry a woman he doesn't want. Their union is forbidden but their chemistry is off the charts.

When she loses everything, her secret love becomes her secret weapon, and the pampered princess becomes a mafia queen.

Bianca Barnes grew up with the world at her feet. She lived a sheltered life with a doting father who provided for her every need. Weeks after his death, her slithering uncle stole her family's fortune and left her penniless.

But she's not taking it lying down.

She'll get her revenge and take back what belongs to her.

She has a plan and a secret weapon who knows how to fight dirty.

Divo Talerico grew up far from Park Avenue.

As the eldest son of a mafia don, everyone expects him to take over his father's position, marry an ally's daughter and take on the most powerful don in Manhattan.

But Divo has other plans.

He'll take his throne. He'll have his uptown girl.
And together they'll make their own way.

CHAPTER 1
DIVO

THE MEN in my family are notorious for marrying women far out of their league. It's true. The Talerico audacity is legendary, and it's been going on for generations. According to my *nonno*, they still curse my great-grandfather's name in Sicily, and I can't say that I blame them. He may have been the worst of us.

Giuseppe Talerico was tall, dark, handsome, and built like a thoroughbred stallion. Graced with our trademark black hair, dark eyes, and impeccable bone structure, he was popular with the ladies but only had eyes for the hot little mayor's daughter, my great-grandmother, Loretta. Giuseppe followed her everywhere and watched her prance around town in her white summer dresses and peep-toe sandals looking like Sophia Loren, teasing him to the brink of insanity. He had it bad, but he had nothing to offer but a tiny goat farm he inherited from his father. Do you think that put a dent in his plans? Hell, no. He wouldn't let something like that keep him from the woman he loved.

Their attraction was mutual, but their affair was forbidden. For weeks they snuck around, falling in love and promising to marry when he saved enough money to ask for her hand. Unfortunately, her father heard she was spending too much time in Giuseppe's pasture and arranged for her to marry someone more suitable. Life without Loretta was not an option. Giuseppe sold his farm and bought them one-way tickets to New York. They lived happily ever after with a house full of kids in Brooklyn, and their youngest son was my *nonno*, Dino.

Dino was the first in my family to live his life on the wrong side of the law. He started out as muscle for the Romano family and then wormed his way to the top by wooing the don's daughter. He didn't take over---Don Romano had a son of his own, but it was only a matter of time before he was the last man standing.

And he knew when to keep his head down.

My father, Dante Talerico, the first don of the Talerico crime family, was another brazen man who coveted a woman he didn't deserve. My mother, Maria Theresa, was the eighteen-year-old daughter of a New York Congressman and as pretty as a picture when he saw her walking home from school with his band of thugs. I need to hand it to my father---that takes some freaking nerve.

But if he hadn't been such a shameless pervert, I wouldn't be the man I am today. The man built to please this little girl six ways to fucking Sunday. "Back it up, baby. Give Daddy what he wants." I stroke the supple curves of Bianca's voluptuous ass, one of her best features, and nudge the seam of her sex with my cock.

"You're four years older than me..." she whines and gives me a hard time. I love this girl to the moon and back, but I could use a little less sass during sex.

I spank one cheek and feel her flesh ripple under the palm of my hand. "Didn't you make me pretend to be your history professor last week? I don't even want to know the story behind that fantasy, little girl." I sink halfway into her tight pussy, pausing when her velvet walls grip my shaft and make me bottom out. Bianca shudders in a fit of ecstasy and falls to her elbows, lifting her gorgeous ass high like an offering for my enjoyment. "Jesus Christ, Bee...this pussy will be the death of me, baby."

"Daddy! You're too big for your little girl." She wiggles her ass in circles and uses my cock as an amusement ride, sliding off and on in tiny jerks that vibrate straight into my heavy balls. She arches her back and perfects her aim, her speed, keeping the same trajectory as her squeaking moans crescendo into a howling bay that echoes off the walls. I slap my hands onto her hips to hold her steady, then flip her over.

"What kind of nasty shit was that?" As much as I love her burgeoning libido, I'm playing the dom in this scenario. I lift her ankles to my shoulders and drop my gaze to her flushed expression.

"Sorry, you know you make me crazy," she sulks and plays with her nipples, hoping to bend me to her will. For a moment, the sight of her round, pale breasts and tight pink peaks makes me lose my concentration. My dry mouth curves into a silly grin, and my vision blurs before the thundering beat of my heart reminds me my stiff cock is dangling centimeters from her hot pussy.

"Good answer, doll. But that doesn't sound like Daddy's good girl." I slide my shaft between her wet slit and nudge her clit. "Do you think that's the way a good girl behaves?"

She nods defiantly, and it takes every ounce of willpower not to prop her over my knee and give her sweet ass the spanking she craves. Last week she got so hot over a bit of discipline she begged to suck my cock and then emptied my balls in seconds. Is it any wonder this girl is seriously making me consider defying my father for the first time in my life?

Considering? No, my mind is made up. Bianca is the only girl for me and if the old man disowns me, so be it.

I shake my head until she stops and follows my lead. Our eyes lock in a heated gaze that makes my heart thump in my ears. I fucking love when she's naked and sweaty. She takes my breath away. "No, b...but..."

"But nothing." I hold my cock against my abdomen and swing it down, slapping her clit with the head of my shaft. She jumps. Her eyes widen with avarice. I do it again and again, slapping, bumping, sliding through her dripping folds until her twisting body snaps and the building tension between us has nowhere to go but home.

"Daddy likes his doll to behave," I rasp, my voice heavy with lust. "And if she can't do it on her own, he'll have to teach her a lesson." I position my cock at her entrance and plow all the way in, filling her to the hilt and reclaiming every space that belongs to me. Her high-pitched squeal starts my undoing, "I'll behave! I'll be good."

The bed shakes, rattling against the wall as I lean forward with the driving force of a battering ram. Her legs lock behind my back. Our hands clasp and settle over her head. "You know Daddy's addicted to this tight little pussy. Why do you give me reasons to punish you?"

"I love when Daddy punishes me with his cock," she whimpers, trembling as her hips roll through every beastly plunge of my cock. "It's the only thing that turns me into a good girl." She lifts her knees, and I sink deeper, panting as her tight walls contract around my steel length.

"Aww, baby, stop teasing me. You're going to make me come too fast. Let me enjoy this pussy a little longer," I plead and dive into her full lips. My hips piston into hers, driving, thrusting harder, faster as the rising tension begins to splinter. Bianca's breath labors. Her thighs shiver, core flexing around my cock as tiny shudders grip her vibrating limbs.

"Daddy!" Bianca sobs through kisses and grips the sheets, bouncing aimlessly as she loses control. "Such a good girl." I dig my hands into her round ass and plunge deep into her clenching sex, thrusting with purpose, railing, fucking my girl like the animal I've become since the day we met. She brings it out in me. All I want to do is take care of my princess---the perfect doll that landed on my lap and somehow fell in love with me. "Are you ready for Daddy's come, baby girl?" I swell inside her, jerking, rutting, mating my woman with a savage desire that twists me in knots and makes me see stars.

"Yes! Give it to me! Give it to me, damn it!" Her inner walls strangle me, milking rope after rope of cum from my thrusting cock. Arousal douses our thighs. Sweat gathers between our writhing bodies. I bring my lips to Bianca's and mumble the only words I can utter, "Mine. You're mine, baby. All fucking mine."

She sinks her teeth into my bottom lip and gives it a slight tug. "Are you certain you're mine?"

I hold her face in my hands and kiss her hard, trying to reassure her of my love and my fidelity. She knows my father's plans are not my own, and I'm trying my best to get out of it with the least amount of collateral damage. "I'm yours, Bee. You know I am. I'm going fucking crazy trying to fix this without cutting off my family, but in the end, I'll do what I need to do. I'm not living the rest of my life without you. I don't even want to think about it."

"Because I'm placing my heart in your hands." She rolls to her side and curls into a fetal position. The sight nearly breaks my panicked heart. I gather her long, brown hair and slide in beside her, grateful for her patience and over the moon she still loves me.

"I'll always take care of your heart, Bee." I kiss her shoulder and exhale with relief, blissfully in love with the girl of my dreams.

CHAPTER 2
DIVO

EVERYONE ALWAYS UNDERESTIMATES ME. It doesn't hurt my feelings--- I'm used to it. They've done it since I was a kid, and I've learned to use it to my advantage.

When you're the eldest son of the don, people wait on you hand and foot. My old man insisted on it. For years, servants treated me like an invalid and never let me do anything for myself. It was frustrating, but my father was a scary guy, and I didn't know enough about the world to argue with him. Then one day, he realized I hadn't magically learned all these things on my own---I couldn't even tie my own shoes.

From that moment on, he looked at me like I was an idiot. There wasn't anything wrong with me. As soon as someone taught me how to tie my own damn shoes, I was as good as gold, but he never shook that initial disappointment. Eventually, he found ways to work through his pain.

Divo doesn't need to be book smart. He's cunning, like an animal.

Thank goodness I'm better looking than my younger brother, or he may have pushed me to the back of the line. The old man appreciates good window dressing, and a handsome son makes him look good in front of the other dons.

Let them believe whatever they like. It's always easier to outwit your enemies when they think you're missing a few gears. I know who I am, and I know what I bring to the table. Besides, only one person's opinion matters, and she makes me feel like I'm the tallest, strongest, most brilliant, most handsome, and by far the luckiest man alive. One day I'll become the man Bianca Barnes sees when she looks at me, but I'm not there yet. I haven't proven my worth and secured the future we want. There's no doubt in my mind we'll be together forever. The alternative is not an option. I'll climb mountains and cross valleys to be with my girl. And right now, there is no greater obstacle to my plans than my father.

He's my Mount Everest.

Years ago, my father made an alliance with Don Giovanni Lombardo, an equally ambitious man with one of the prettiest daughters in Manhattan. Gala Lombardo doesn't hold a candle to my Bee, but our fathers thought we'd make the perfect match. They sealed their pledge by arranging our marriage for the year Gala turns twenty, and once upon a time, I might have considered going through with it. But that was before I fell in love with Bianca. That was before I saw my doll across a crowded dance floor, felt the earth come to a crashing halt, heard the angels sing, and felt my heart beat in double time. My feet moved before my brain could register what was happening. Meeting her changed the game---it changed my life. I knew then that I'd have to find a way to get out of the arrangement. There would be no other woman in my future. Bianca would be my one and only wife.

But you don't just say no to my father. He's not the type of man who listens to reason. And the more I fall in love with my girl, the more desperate I've become to find a way out of this fucking mess. She's left me once before, and I was lucky enough to beg and crawl my way back into her life.

Fortunately, I'm fairly certain Gala doesn't want me any more than I want her. Some guys in my position would do their family's bidding, marry the woman their father picks, and simply keep a mistress on the side. There's no fucking way I'd make my doll the other woman. She's too good to come second to anyone, and frankly, my dick belongs to her. I refuse to give it to anyone else.

My friends like to say I'm whipped by a Park Avenue princess but I'm not ashamed to admit Bianca owns me. She owns my heart. She owns my cock. And you better believe I own her. Every inch of that girl belongs to me.

"Divo, we need to talk." My father's imposing figure guards the hallway into the kitchen. I should have known it was a trap and used the back entrance, although there's little doubt that he has men posted there. Whenever he wants to catch me off guard, he asks my mother to call me home. He knows I won't make excuses or delay if she asks me to stop for a visit.

I look over my shoulder at my men, Nico and Joey, then turn back to my father. Fearing the worst, I swallow the lump in my throat before answering. The last thing I want to do is show weakness or vulnerability when I feel it the most. "Can they stay, or is this a private conversation?"

He shrugs with indifference and instructs us to follow him into the kitchen. "They can hear what I have to say. Soon everyone will know."

I tread lightly behind him and feel my heart somersault into my stomach. I hear a familiar voice commiserating with my mother from inside the kitchen, and bile rises into my throat. It's Mrs. Lombardo. The Lombardos are here. Why the hell are they here?

"Divo!" Mrs. Lombardo throws her arms around me and gives me a kiss on each cheek, smearing hot pink lipstick on my face. Behind her, my mother stifles a cringe and then approaches me with a wet napkin to wipe me down. I know she disagrees with this, but she's grown tired of arguing with my father.

"Sit down, Divo. We have news." My father kicks a chair in my direction and commands me to sit. He grins from ear to ear and pours me a glass of Prosecco. My first instinct is to wave it off. It's too early, and this doesn't feel like anything I'll want to celebrate. Giovanni takes a glass and hands one to his wife. They toast before anyone's spoken, much to my father's chagrin. My mother stands behind me and places her hands on my shoulders, petting me like her favorite poodle to soothe my nerves.

"What's this about?" I play the idiot. They'd expect that from me, and since our wedding is still two years away, I'm not sure why they're corking the bubbly so soon.

My father pats my bicep and holds out his goblet, clinking it with the glass I haven't touched. "I probably should have told you last week but you've been a pain in the ass to reach. We've decided to push your wedding date to a week from Saturday at Saint Catherine's Cathedral. The plans are in motion and the Lombardos are busy with the arrangements and wedding invitations have gone out. Gala's a beautiful girl, son. I know you'll be happy once you get used to one another."

I stare, confused, befuddled and absolutely horrified at the four adults celebrating the marriage I don't want. "That's the whole point. Gala's a little girl. She just turned eighteen," I stammer, dumbstruck with the outrageous turn of events. "Why now? You said two years. It was always set for after her twentieth birthday. What happened?"

"Enzo Lupo has gained far too much power. You should have seen him acting like Julius Cesar at the wedding on Friday. He practically made a pass at your fiancée, simply to rub it in our faces. We need to show a united front, and we're not the only families forming unions. The Russos and Marinos just joined hands, and Giovanni assures me--" I cut him off, fearing he's lost his marbles. This can't be his idea. My father's mental health has been slowly deteriorating over the last year. It's a well-kept secret, but he's become easier to manipulate. I fear Lombardo is using my father's men to exact vengeance against Lupo for imaginary slights that have nothing to do with us.

"Pop, the Russos and Marinos have their heads so far Lupo's ass they could polish his tonsils. Rosalie Russo is three months pregnant. Of course, Paul Marino married her. Her father would kill him if he didn't. Their marriage is not a political alliance." I look to my mother and plead with her to reason with him.

Giovanni glares at me, hoping I'll pipe down before my father regains his senses.

"Dante, weddings cost money, and last-minute arrangements are twice as expensive. Most of our money is tied up in investments right now." My mother tries her best to rein him in, but my father pulls her into his lap and dismisses her with a kiss on the cheek.

"Maria, you're always worried about the details. This is our eldest son's wedding. We'll figure out the expenses, my love. We should toast." He lifts his glass. The Lombardos chant toasts in Italian. No doubt, Gala Lombardo is somewhere panicked out of her mind. And across town, my doll is looking up lasagna recipes to surprise me for dinner.

Without a word, I push my chair away from the table, rise from my seat and turn away from my parents. My pulse clamors with rage. My fists clench at my sides, and my eyes scan the hallway for an acceptable target to punch. Bianca's going to kill me. She won't understand, and I can't fault her if she threatens to leave me again.

I need to speak to Gala and I need to come clean to Bee. No matter the consequences, she deserves the gory details.

I can only hope she understands and believes I won't let her down.

My men follow me out, matching my heavy footfalls as we march through the stained-glass mahogany door and leave my parent's home in a wave of simmering rage. My fury fizzles into fear when I glimpse the spectacle on the street. Outside, a line of black sedans idle near my car. Four goons with holstered guns clearly visible in the light of day exit two vehicles and head in our direction.

"Jesus Christ, what the shit did you do? Those are Lupo's men." Nico freezes and tries his best to make himself smaller, shielding himself behind my back. He's a terrible bodyguard.

"I don't know. But I have a feeling I'm about to find out. If I don't make it, please, tell Bianca what happened to me." I step forward and resign myself to fate. There's no running from Enzo Lupo.

CHAPTER 3
BIANCA

"ALL RIGHT, in five minutes, I want you to get the lasagna out of the oven and make sure you use both gloves this time. Remove the foil and then slide it back in for another twenty-five minutes. Don't forget to set the timer." My best friend's boyfriend, Lance, wipes the kitchen counters while his doting girlfriend, my bestie, Tara, unfastens his apron. It's so nice to see her so happy. Their relationship is still brand-spanking new, but the way they love on each other, you'd think they've been together for years.

I clap my hands and fight the urge to open the oven, opting instead to squat down for a peek. "It smells scrumptious. He'll never believe I did this on my own. Last week's pizza was barely edible." Poor Divo tried to make it himself, but I insisted I wanted to learn. No one ever taught me how to cook, and ever since I lost all my money, I've tried my best to become more self-sufficient. When my earlier batch of lasagna came out like cardboard, Tara phoned in reinforcements. Lance is a bonafide Cuisine Channel chef, and although Italian isn't his specialty, he swore he's made it since he was a kid.

Tara pours us each a glass of Pinot Noir and hops backward onto a barstool. "I don't believe Divo gives a damn about your cooking." She wags her eyebrows and takes a generous sip of wine. "And if he's spending the night tonight, I may have to stay with Lance. You two get mighty rowdy."

My cheeks catch fire under her sassy gaze. "Oh, no! Please, don't go. This is your place, and I'm making you uncomfortable in your own house."

She waves her hand and gestures for me to stop making a fuss. "Oh, God, Bee. I'm only kidding--"

Lance bumps her hip with his and interrupts her apology. "Don't listen to her. She's kidding, and she's got one hell of a set of pipes herself." He gives Tara a stern gaze, and she smothers a tiny giggle with a sip of wine. "We've had this planned for days. I'm cooking her dinner, and we're catching up on one of the latest shows she's streaming."

"You're too kind, but I know I've overstayed my welcome. These job interviews have become one colossal joke after another. My Uncle Geoffrey blackballed me all over town, and I don't have enough money in savings to pay a decent lawyer the required retainer to take him on. I'm sure he counted on that. It might be time for me to think about visiting my nonna in Florence." I can hardly speak the words for fear once I put them out in the universe, I'll place them in motion. Maybe I'm being childish and naïve, but Divo's one of the few good things I have left in my life. Besides Tara, he's the only person who didn't abandon me when I lost everything.

"And leave Divo?" Tara covers her gasp with her hand. "I told you I'd lend you the money, sweetie. I can ask my parents tomorrow. Your uncle stole your inheritance, your father's legacy, and your home. Everyone knows how much your dad loved you. He would've never cut you out of his will."

I shake my head and pull on my oven mitts. "No. I won't take your money. Geoff is using the best law firm on the east side. If I lose, I won't be able to repay you, and I'll be even deeper in the hole. You've been generous enough." I lift the lasagna dish off the rack and set it on the stove. Lance steps forward and fights the temptation to give me a hand, but I quickly unwrap the foil and slide it back into the oven. Divo's due to arrive in thirty minutes, and I want everything to be perfect. Maybe he'll take the news about Florence easier on a full stomach.

"I'll lend you money, Bianca. I have extra savings to spare. If this Geoffrey guy is as conniving as Tara says, it will be my pleasure." Lance digs into his back pocket and produces his business card. "It could be a loan or gift. If it rights a wrong, then it's worth it. Please email me if you change your mind."

Tears of gratitude render me speechless. The last four months have been nothing less than an inverted emotional roller coaster dangling me upside down while simultaneously spinning my life out of control. Two weeks after I met the love of my life, my father died. We'd only been together a short while, but Divo's love helped soothe my broken heart and his tenderness in my hour of grief made me more determined to keep him in my life. I know what he does, and it isn't easy loving a dangerous man, but that's not the side I know or love. I've already pushed him out of my life once---when I found out about his father's plans to marry him to someone else---and our three-day separation drove me into an abyss of unfathomable despair. I'm not sure I can do it again.

Divo's love held me together when I felt alone in the world, but just when things settled down, the rollercoaster took an ugly turn.

On the day we buried my father, his half-brother, a man I'd met twice in my life, produced an alternate copy of my father's will. The new document that no one had ever seen before left him everything. According to his attorneys, they visited shortly before his death, and Geoffrey claimed my father signed everything to him to make up for past wrongs.

He and Geoffrey shared the same mother, but my grandmother left my grandfather to marry a man she met on a beach in Fort Lauderdale. My father lived with my wealthy grandfather in New York and rarely saw his mother, who lived with her new family in Florida. I know he tried to befriend his younger brother on several occasions, but my uncle had no interest in seeing my dad unless he was handing out money.

My father was young, but he knew he was dying. It pained him dearly to leave me behind, and he showed me his last will and testament less than a week before his passing. He wanted me to know he'd always take care of me---even when he wasn't around anymore. I was his only child and heir, and there were no provisions for Geoffrey. I know in my heart of hearts he would not have changed it without telling me, and if he did, there is no way he would have left everything to my uncle.

But none of that mattered.

Geoffrey's crooked attorneys filed motions to seize my inheritance, assets, home, and even trust fund. Fortunately, the last-minute confusion froze the entire estate, granting neither of us access to my father's personal accounts. He didn't predict that. No doubt he planned to raid my father's billions and buy an island in the Caribbean. Now he needs to work for a paycheck. I'm broke, but Geoff's shady maneuvering gave him access to my father's company, giving him enough capital to keep me away from that will.

In three months, he has yet to give me access to the original copy of the altered will. And I know it's fake. I just need to prove it.

I release the shaky breath building up in my lungs and place Lance's card on the counter. "I appreciate your friendship and love you for offering, but I could never accept this kind of help. Things are hard now, and I'll find a way to fix it, but I'd rather you use your money on the less fortunate. I might not be rich, but I'm a lucky girl with a roof over my head and more options than most. I'll figure this out."

Tara hops off the stool and walks toward me with her arms spread wide. "Stop acting like you're in this all alone, damn it. I've got your back. And if I've got your back, my man's got your back." She hugs me tightly, rocking me back and forth, then spins me into the living room.

"I love it when you call me your man," Lance hums with excitement and smiles from ear to ear.

"Aww, shucks, you love everything." Tara leans back and lets him plant a kiss on her forehead. "And we're off! You've got the house to yourself. Have a good time with Divo, and let us know what he thinks of the lasagna. I'm sure Lance will be waiting on pins and needles to hear his review." She gives me a final hug, grabs her bag, and heads to the door. I give her a thumbs up and peek into the oven, psyched to see the cheese bubbling and browning to perfection.

"Bee! Divo's here! And it looks like he got into a fight." Tara calls from the foyer. I check the time and unfasten the messy apron covering my dress. He wasn't due for another fifteen minutes, and I haven't had a chance to freshen up.

"Divo!" I rush into the hall, straightening my clothes and brushing my hair with my fingers. "You're early." I gasp at the sight of Divo's bruised and bloodied face. My fists clench at my sides, my spine steels with fury that someone injured the man I love. His disheveled hair and clothes have traces of dust and blood, like he's been tossed or kicked to the ground.

"What happen!" I fly into his arms and press my lips gently to his, desperate to soothe whatever ache he feels but careful not to place too much pressure on his swollen lip.

"It doesn't matter, baby. I'm here with you." He molds his mouth to mine, burning my lips with a fiery kiss that makes me forget everything but this moment. I fall into his embrace and climb his body, winding my legs around his hips until we're locked tightly together, two bodies sealed, bound, hopeless without the other. But I can't let this go. There's something wrong in his world, and in his world, people die.

His legs move beneath me, carrying us towards the back of the house, towards the scent of the food. I whisper through kisses, "Talk to me, Divo. I made lasagna but you don't have to eat if you're in pain."

He hums, kissing me slowly, licking my lips but mumbling something that needs to be said. There's something on his mind and it's more than pain or fist fights.

But whatever it is, he doesn't want to say it.

"Divo?" I pull away and lift my gaze, searching his eyes for some sign of the truth.

"Let's eat sweetheart. I don't want your hard work to go to waste. It looks worse than it feels. Just give me a chance to clean up and I'll tell you everything."

CHAPTER 4
BIANCA

ON EVERY ROLLERCOASTER, there's a point on the ride---after you've been shaken and battered, dipped, then jerked---when the line of cars climbs the highest peak in a slow ascent that often overlooks some of the most scenic views of the park. I think it's meant to throw you off guard. You know something terrible is coming. Of course, it is. You're on a rollercoaster, for heaven's sake, and as long as you're strapped in, the ride isn't over. For a moment, the car stills, and you take in the view. But you know the worst is coming, and you brace yourself by holding on as tight as you can before the final drop---the freefall that makes your heart leap out of your chest and your lunch bounce into your throat. That's what I've been doing the last two months--- waiting for the freefall.

"Please, say something, Bee. I know it sounds fucking horrible, but I have a plan to fix this." Divo's mouth moves in slow motion, every word gradually unraveling the rug he's yanked from under my feet. Wedding invitations are circu- lating New York City engraved with Divo's name and Gala Lombardo, a woman I've never met but whose future husband I've apparently been banging for the last four months. How can I trust him? He promised it wouldn't come to this, yet here we are.

"You...you need to leave." I shake my head and awaken from my catatonic daze with a shudder. The fork in my hand, previously hovering mid-air, lands on a lumpy pile of ricotta and splatters marinara sauce on my white dress. "Divo, I need you to leave. Forget my name. Forget my number. Forget we ever met!" I spring out of my chair, and my icy exterior falters. My fractured heart shatters and pulls the air from my lungs. Sobs burst free, tumbling out from my clenched throat in gulping wails as my knees weaken, and I hold the table to keep me steady.

"Baby, I'm not going anywhere." Divo knocks over his chair and jumps to his feet, catching my waist before my knees buckle and take me to the carpet. "Please, don't make me go, Bee. I love you. I'm not marrying her. My father could hold a gun to my head, and he still couldn't make me recite vows to anyone but you."

I want to believe him. I don't hear an ounce of duplicity in his voice. It sounds ridiculous after so much back and forth, but I know he loves me---I just can't listen. There were never any guarantees when we fell in love. We stood the same chance as any other love affair, and with so many obstacles in our way, maybe this has finally run its course. "I can't hear anymore. It's over. Marry her. Don't marry her. Do what you please. Just leave me alone and let me move on with my life." I wrench my arms out from his embrace and stumble away, clutching the walls to guide me as far from him as I can get.

"Bee!" his pained growl makes me hiccup through crashing tears. I race to the stairs and swing on the banister, stomping away in a frenzy to the sound of his advancing steps.

"Go away!" I quicken my pace, charging faster to the second floor and circling the landing towards the third. "How can I ever believe anything you say? Do you think I'm a fool?"

"Baby.." his voice breaks as he reaches out to catch me, missing me by inches.

"Do not *baby* me, Divo Talerico. I am done with you. How would you feel if there were wedding invitations with my name and...and...and...Hugo Chamberlain? Huh? You'd spit nails!" I scream and deliberately toss out a name he's unfamiliar with to piss him off.

He gasps like a girl and leaps across the hall, catching my arm before I disappear into my room. "Who the hell is Hugo Chamberlain?"

"Just a man who happens to be none of your damn business. Don't assume for one second I'll end up alone, mister. Go be with your Gala, and let me move on," I shriek as I wrestle out of his iron grasp, wiggling and crawling into my bedroom while he holds on to my legs.

"I don't want Gala. You're my woman. You're the only woman I want." He yanks off my shoes and tosses them over my head. "You didn't let me finish the story, baby. There's no way I'm going through with it, but even if my mind wasn't already made up, she plans to run away the night of our rehearsal dinner." He kisses my calves and licks his way up my thighs.

"Oh, no, you don't! I know what you're doing! And what do you mean rehearsal? How can you let it get that far?" I thrash my legs and fight to kick him loose. It doesn't work. He's too strong, and my effort is minimal at best.

"My eye, Bee. Watch my eye," he whines for sympathy to make me stop wiggling, then slips my panties down my legs.

"Goddamn it, Divo..." I claw the carpet and crawl away, hoping to regroup my thoughts before falling under his spell. Within seconds my crusade proves fruitless. Divo slides beneath me, wedges his shoulders between my thighs, and lifts my pussy straight onto his mouth. He swipes his tongue through my wet heat and strikes my swollen bud, always ready for his touch. He suckles, lashing my clit with brutal strokes that make me sing through curses, damning him to hell while he primes my pussy for his cock.

"I hate you..." I moan, losing focus as my arms fall to my side and my thighs spread wider. My heart and body succumb with ease, but my mind puts up a valiant fight. "You need to leave..." I rock back and forth, sliding my pussy against his face as smothered screams eke out through my chattering teeth. I'm hopeless.

"No, baby. Don't say that. I fucking love you."

"You said you wouldn't break my heart," I moan through tears, scared to death of trusting him but unable to break away now.

"Never. Never. Never, baby. I'll never break your heart. We'll be together forever, Bee." He eases me onto his lap and slams his thick cock inside me. The air leaves my lungs in a loud whoosh. I catch my breath and settle into his length, wrapping my legs around his waist. I cling tightly, grinding into every vicious thrust and relishing the twisted mix of pain and pleasure it brings.

"I won't be your mistress," I vow as his frenzied thrusts lift me higher and higher, each plunge grazing my clit and tightening the coil winding within my core. Shudders of ecstasy roll through my quivering limbs as he takes me hard, bouncing and fucking me with wild-eyed madness until my pussy spasms around his cock and I feel his hot seed fill every space inside me.

"You'll never come second, Bianca. Never."

CHAPTER 5
DIVO

"THIS IS the best lasagna I've ever tasted, sweetheart. It's better than my mother's and *nonna's*. You outdid yourself." I wipe the last of my second plate with a piece of garlic bread and hum with pleasure, savoring every bite.

Bianca's cheeks glow with the rosy hue of bashful pride, but a hint of sadness lingers in her big brown eyes. She folds her legs, crossing them beneath her thighs, and slouches forward on the kitchen tile. It's 2:00am, and neither of us can sleep. My stomach wouldn't stop growling with hunger, and no doubt, thoughts of murdering me in my sleep kept her awake most of the night. If she knew how much I loved her, she'd know there's no way I would marry another woman. And it's my fault for making her doubt me.

"Thank you. I had help. Tara's boyfriend was here earlier and gave me a few tips." She hugs her chest and stares at the floor, unable to look me in the eye.

I set my plate on the counter over my head and extend my hand, hoping she'll take my invitation to sit closer. She glares at my hand, hesitating or thinking about her next move. Bianca isn't a fly by the seat of her pants kind of girl. That's one of the things I love about her. My world is chaos. I never know which end is up or down. Danger might feel sexy to some, but too much instability wears on your soul. When I come home to Bee, everything's made right. She takes all the balls I'm juggling, puts them in a box, labels them, files them away, and dusts the crazy world off my shoulders until tomorrow. She's the first real home I've ever had, and Satan himself couldn't drag me away from my girl.

"Divo..." she whispers and walks her fingers into my palm. I close my hand around hers and guide her into my lap, cradling her gently until she rests her head on my chest. "Maybe we need a break until you get things in order. I could go to Florence. My grandmother could use the company. Maybe she'll lend me the money to hire attorneys who aren't afraid to challenge my uncle's lawyers and that famous handwriting expert from Switzerland to refute the liar working for him."

Florence? Italy? No, Italy is filled with Italians, and I know from personal experience my doll's dark hair and sharp curves would be far too much temptation for swarthy men trolling the Tuscan countryside with their tight white pants and windswept hair. I don't need that kind of competition. They'll pretend they don't know English and hope a miscommunication gets them into her pants. Bianca's hardly a pushover, but sometimes she's just too nice for her own good.

"Not Florence, sweetheart. I know you didn't want my help, and I've tried to respect your wishes, but enough is enough. You've tried being civil with your uncle when we both know he's nothing but a criminal. You're used to gentle people who do what they say, check all the boxes, say thank you, and please. They're not innocent, but they do the right thing because they're afraid they'll be kicked out of high society." Her eyes flicker wide as she considers my words then she nods with resignation. I lean forward and plant a kiss on her nose. Bee wants to believe the best in everyone, and the sooner she shakes off her gullibility, the sooner we can get to work.

"If I can just get the will, there really isn't anything he can do." She nuzzles her face into my neck and exhales with a sigh. I wind my arms around her, wondering how on earth I made someone so innocent and sweet fall in love with me. Bianca knows what I do for a living, but I've always kept the details to a minimum. It's standard operating procedure not to let the women in our lives know the true nature of our criminal activities to keep them safe and keep that part of our world separate from our home life.

But Bianca's different. If I want her to place her faith in me, I need to trust her.

"Do you love me, sweetheart? Knowing what I am and what I do---could you spend your life with me?" I ask the question that's weighed on my heart since I first fell in love with Bianca. She might be part Italian, but she's not from my neighborhood and not part of my world. She grew up with butlers, chauffeurs, nannies, and private schools in circles full of socialites, celebrities, and politicians. I grew up with criminals on streets where everyone strove to become a mobster because that's how you became someone. I'm a selfish bastard for dragging her into my seedy life, but so help me, God, once I got a taste of my girl, I couldn't live without her.

"I won't pretend it doesn't scare me, but I'd be lost without you," she whispers and lets her lips trace the skin over my heart, kissing me once before lifting her gaze to mine. "I love you."

"Don't go to Florence. Stay here and fight for what's yours. I'll help you. The guy who beat me up--" She squirms out of my arms and sits in front of me, recalling I never finished telling her the story of my wounds.

"Who beat you up? You promised you'd tell me." Her

brows pinch with anger as she examines the cut on my fore-head. "Did he sneak up on you? Are you going after him?" She grabs a napkin and douses it with water, wiping down the last droplets of blood matting my eyebrow to get a better look.

I shake my head and nestle her into my lap. "No, sweet-heart, the man who did this to me isn't someone I can go after. But he is someone who can help us."

She stares, confused and rightly so. "That doesn't make any sense. Why would this guy beat you up then help you?"

"I told you my father is a don, right?"

She nods, stops to think, then nods again. "Like Marlon Brando in the Godfather?"

I sigh with exasperation but understand he's most people's only reference to La Cosa Nostra. "Yes, like Marlon Brando, but much smaller potatoes. My dad is more like the guy in the white suit in the second movie, but I digress. Beyond people like Don Corleone, there's always someone who rises to the top and wields so much power he becomes the don of dons---the head honcho."

Her eyes grow as wide as saucers. "And that's who beat you up?"

I lean my forehead into hers, fearing I've frightened her. "His name is Enzo Lupo, and he's in love with Gala Lombardo. He beat me up to make me cancel the wedding, but I told him I had no intention of going through with it. He said if I cooperated, he'd help me take over my father's role. I love my dad, but he's not in his right mind, and Gala's father is taking advantage of him. The sooner I take over, the sooner I can help you deal with your fucking uncle, baby. And with Enzo's help, that motherfucker won't know what hit him."

"But...but Divo, you're talking about using mobsters to scare..." She stops and shifts her gaze from side to side, considering her options. "Do you think it would work?"

"Fuck, yes. Enough bullshit. You're my girl. And no one

fucks with my girl. Except me, baby." I wrap her legs around my waist, push her panties to one side and wedge my cock inside her tight pussy. "I love you, Bianca. You're my fucking queen."

CHAPTER 6
DIVO

I GROAN, shuddering loudly as I dip my face into a sink of ice and try to numb the shooting pain from my eye sockets down to my jaw. The Toscano brothers, Enzo Lupo's twin bodyguards, stand on opposite ends of the mirror with their typical stone-faced expressions. Both appear unmoved by the grunts and cries coming from the other side of the bathroom door. A few minutes ago, it was me. Now Enzo violently takes out his frustrations on his cousin and underboss, Bruno. I'm thrilled. He's the reason Bianca will surely have a heart attack when I walk through her door tonight.

Enzo Lupo has fallen hard for eighteen-year-old Gala Lombardo. He's twice her age, and if you ask me, he's way too fucking old for her. But no one's asking me. I'm not sure he's ever been in a serious relationship, but there's no doubt he's got it bad for her. He's about to jeopardize his empire and shake up fragile alliances to take her for himself.

As instructed, I sent Bruno a message notifying Enzo about Gala's plans to run away. He said he wanted to help her. It's self-serving, but it's the only way for all three of us to get what we want. She plans to run away during the rehearsal, but I know for a fact her family is on to her. If he wants to intercede, he has a small window. Any delay could risk an all-out war. When I never heard back from him, I sent seven more. I knew something had to be wrong. Earlier today, I learned Enzo never received them. In a fit of rage, he brought me here and beat the shit out of me.

Lucky for me, I know how to take a beating.

I lift my head at the sound of footsteps and stare into the mirror. Enzo appears at the door, his blue eyes wide with a subtle look of remorse. He claps his hands and forces an awkward smile. "I apologize for..." He looks over his shoulder into the other room and points.

I shove a handful of ice into a towel, hold it over my face, and then draw my hand to my forehead, shielding my swollen eyes from the blinding lights overhead. "I can't see that far."

He winces, then snaps his fingers at Michael Toscano. "Will you get him a chair, for fuck's sake?" Michael waves his hand at his brother Matteo who marches into the other room, pulls the chair from under Bruno's ass, and carries it in over his head.

"Please sit," Enzo rasps, his voice heavy with shame. "Again, I apologize for my temper. Bruno will get a second beating later today for sitting on your messages and not saying a word while I took my anger out on your face. My doctor's on his way to tend to your wounds, but if you feel the need to see your own physician, send the bills to me. I'm horribly ashamed of myself." He runs his hands through his tousled hair and paces in front of me. "Divo, I need you to play along tonight. I'll reward you handsomely when you take over as don. Your father will never know you helped me."

He offers his hand as a sign of friendship, and I don't hesitate to take it. "They're expecting her to run. They've had a spy watching her all week. I only found out who it was on my way here. You'll need to stage a distraction to give her time to escape through the side exit."

He nods and wrings his hands with anxiety. "It's Serafina, right? I was wondering why she'd taken such a special interest in Gala. Don't worry. I'll get Michael and Matteo to keep her distracted during dinner. They can be very charming." The twins groan and then silently resign themselves to Lupo's orders.

"Don't mind them. I'll reward the twins for their troubles. And I'll reward you. I know your father isn't well, and I'm prepared to back you when Lombardo makes a play for Talerico territory. That's been his game plan all along---to pounce when the don is weak. That's why you're so important. He can't claim it if you're not married to his daughter." His words sink into my fuzzy brain and fill in the missing piece of the puzzle. That lowlife piece of trash thought he could take what was mine? Un-fucking-believable.

First Bianca's uncle and now Giovanni Lombardo---two sides of the same coin.

"Enzo, I need a favor. I know it places me in your debt, but it concerns the woman I love and the man who took everything from her. I need to help her get back what she lost." I appeal to him as a man in love and hope he takes the bait.

He cocks his head to one side and rubs his hand across his five o'clock shadow. "Don't mention it. I owe you a favor for what I did to your face, and if my plan proves successful, I will forever be in your debt. Please, tell me what you need. I'm at your service."

CHAPTER 7
BIANCA

THE ADDRESS on the card reads 36 River Terrace, and according to Google maps, it faces Rockefeller Park and the Hudson River. I researched the location last night before bed, and I've decided to take it as a good omen. Divo and I met here in Tribeca. It was a lucky once-in-a-lifetime chance that never would have come to fruition if Tara hadn't dragged me out of the house and forced me out for a night of dancing.

I hadn't been out in ages. My father's illness took up most of my free time, and I dreaded spending nights away from home. I didn't want to miss a thing.

But that night, Tara pleaded, and my father convinced me to spend some time letting my hair down and blowing off steam. It was the hottest new dance club, the one everyone fought to get into---but all I wanted to do was go home. Fifteen minutes in, I whined for a reprieve. Thirty minutes later and she promised we'd go after one more dance.

That's when I saw him.

Tall, broad, clearly jacked, and busting out from his tailored suit, a black-haired god with brilliant hazel eyes parted the crowd like Moses and floated towards me on a cloud. His smile bewitched me. The deep vibrations of his sultry voice sent shivers down my spine and made my thighs clench with a trembling ache that only his cock could quench.

That night we danced until the lights came on. The following night we made love for the first time. I had no experience and no expectations, but Divo took me by surprise. He ravaged my body with such mind-shattering finesse he stole my heart. And he's had it ever since.

"We're here, Miss Barnes," Vincenzo, the driver Enzo Lupo sent to Tara's house at 9:00am on the dot, calls from the front and exits the car, straightening his suit as he walks to the back. He flings open my door and offers his hand to help me out from the backseat. "Mr. Ponti's office will be on the tenth floor. The receptionist knows to page me when you're almost done." He gives me a wink and points to the front doors of Enzo Lupo's enclave, headquarters to the legitimate side of his business.

I hop out of the car and speed walk as fast as my legs can take me in my poorly chosen pencil skirt. I zip across the crowded plaza, zigzagging through happy families, tourists, commuters, and dog walkers on their way to the park. I feel exposed and judged like everyone knows I'm headed into a mob building. In the distance, a muffler backfires, and I duck, imagining FBI agents littering my body with bullets on my way to my new attorney's office. As I reach the building, a couple with a baby stroller exits through an automatic door, and I weave past them into the lobby, sick to my stomach and panting through labored breaths.

"Why are you sweating?" Divo places his hands on my shoulders and spins me to face him. "I watched you from here. You looked insane."

I fall into his arms and lean my head into his chest. "How do you do it? I felt eyes on me everywhere. Cops on every corner---CIA, FBI, Homeland Security, you name it." I pull on his lapels and shake him with panic.

"Holy shit, baby. You're visiting a lawyer about a will. You don't have to get involved with the ugly side if you don't want to, but you're done being a good girl. Antonio Ponti is Enzo's lawyer. Everyone in Manhattan, including your uncle's fancy boys, know he's Enzo's lawyer. And do you know what that means?" Divo hugs my shoulders and whisks me into a private elevator.

"He's good?" I hold him close and breathe a sigh of relief I let him join me. I thought it was something I needed to do alone—recapturing my dignity and righting family wrongs. But Divo convinced me he wanted to be around for all of it. I admit I was skeptical about using a mob lawyer and, for a few moments, downright terrified, but I'm beginning to see the error of my ways. This is a gift from Enzo Lupo---an apology for smashing Divo's face last week. I'd typically never accept favors from a known kingpin, especially one as powerful as Lupo, but times are hard. I'm still furious, but I appreciate the sentiment and figure he owes us after what he did to my man. Besides, I'm already in bed with Divo, literally and figuratively, and there's no going back now.

The underworld is shifting. Their power structure is currently in flux. Whether I like it or not, Divo's deeply rooted in this world, and from now on, so am I.

Where he goes, I go.

Divo smiles and kisses my hand. "He is good, but there aren't many lawyers who have Enzo's army behind them. He'll get that will, Bee. If it exists, Tony Ponti will hold him down while Enzo's goons pull it out of his ass." He chuckles and stands against the sliding doors, keeping them open for me to pass through. "I mean if it comes to that."

CHAPTER 8
BIANCA

"YOU'RE BEING UNREASONABLE, Bee. You're twenty-two years old and not qualified to run a company like Barnes, Incorporated." My late father's half-brother and usurper of my birthright, Geoffrey ignores his lawyer's instructions and addresses me with his usual cocky bluster.

"My name is Bianca...Bianca Barnes." I hiss through gritted teeth and once again remind the other side of the room that I am a Barnes, unlike their client, Geoffrey Kimble.

He pretends to laugh at my remark, then narrows his gaze in my direction, hoping to intimidate me into silence. A month ago, that might have worked. Two months ago, I couldn't stand to be in the same room with him for fear I'd be driven to tears. This is the first time I've had the confidence to push back, and I won't stop here.

"We've been through this before," Geoff interjects and tries to shut the meeting down before it begins. He spreads his arms across the conference table like a performer putting on a show and clears his throat with the promise of words that will wow us into submission. There's no way I'll sit through another one of his festival of lies. I've heard enough from this pompous windbag to last a lifetime.

I cringe and lift both arms like an umpire calling a time-out. "And we'll go through it again, asshole." I'm not used to being rude--- it's never been my style. But Divo's right. The high road is for suckers who like to lose. This prick lost the privilege of courtesy when he stole my money and my father's company. I've come to play hardball and if my hands get dirty—so be it.

My attorney, Antonio Ponti clears his throat like Pavarotti preparing to belt out an opera at the Met. "Zip it, Kimble. My client's heard enough of your bullshit. We want the will you claim her father signed with the original ink, witnessed, notarized, and filed. I don't want to see a photocopy. We've hired two handwriting experts to analyze her father's signature from over twenty samples. My client has requested the original copy since the funeral, and you've ignored a court order. You now have three days." He holds three fingers up for show, then unfolds the judge's order and slides it across the table.

"Don't forget to read it this time, dickhead." Divo unceremoniously tosses the envelope across the table and hits Geoffrey on the forehead.

He balks, spinning his wheels and grumbling profanities under his breath as his face turns beet red. He turns to his lawyers. One after another, men dressed in five-thousand-dollar suits avert their eyes and check the little hand on their Rolex watches. No doubt they've warned him he's in contempt of court. When no one tries to correct me by reciting nonsense precedent, he resorts to the skillful art of manipulation.

"I feel sorry for you, Bee. You're obviously still in mourning." His words of comfort mean nothing. People backed into a corner come out swinging, but I'm one step ahead of him.

"And I feel sorry for you. It must have been horrible to live in my father's shadow your entire life. If only grandma hadn't run off with the cabana boy in Fort Lauderdale, you might have been one of Malcolm Barnes' sons." I straighten my back and brush the hair off my shoulders. I hate to throw my grandmother under the bus, but we only met a few times when I was a little girl, and she wasn't very nice to my dad.

His eye twitches to the same beat as the throbbing vein dancing on his temple. He bristles and stammers to correct me, "My father was not a cabana boy. He was a lifeguard. And as I was saying..."

I cut him off, bored with this song and dance. "That's a fine occupation, and I hardly begrudge grandma a good time, but you never wanted to be my father's brother until you found out he was sick."

"You're only angry because your father chose to cut you out of his will." He takes a punch and misses. No one could make me doubt my father's love.

I shake my head. "That won't work. You just don't understand a parent's love, Geoff. It must have been hard being a burden." Divo stands and helps me out from my seat. Antonio's in no mood to linger. We have reservations at Vinnie's in Little Italy, and he doesn't want to be late. He hasn't stopped bragging about the gnocchi since we left the office.

My uncle's sweaty face twists with rage. Unable to process my defiance, he lunges through the stack of papers and takes a swipe at my arm. Nico and Joey, Divo's two oversized, broad-shouldered bodyguards block his trajectory and send him flying across the room. Antonio isn't having any of it. Like a frustrated headmaster, he points to the Upper East Side attorneys seated on the opposite side of the table and warns them to get their client under control. His stern expression sends them scurrying to Geoffrey's side.

"Basta!" He wipes his brow, exasperated by the lack of respect. "No need to come to us, Mr. Kimble. We'll send someone to your place of business on Friday at precisely 3:00pm. Do not keep my associates waiting and do not try to escape. Please have the necessary paperwork, or we'll be waiting for you at your home on 97th Street." Antonio snaps his fingers, and Divo escorts me towards the door.

"Are you threatening me?" Geoffrey stammers and feigns offense. He didn't expect me to fight back. He thought I'd crawl under a rock or marry a rich old man to reclaim my fortune. I've thrown a massive wrench in his plans.

"This is my card, Mr. Kimble." Antonio drops it on the table and then winks at a nervous lawyer standing by. "Please make sure your client complies or you'll anger my associates. And believe me, you don't want to anger my associates. *Capisce?*"

The frightened lawyer nods once. "Cap... yes, sir."

CHAPTER 9
DIVO

"WHAT DO you mean he got away?" Bee screams at the top of her lungs and throws her arms over her head. The crazed expression on her flushed face is nearly unrecogniz-able---beady eyes, tight lips, and disheveled hair strewn in every direction. She punches the air, kicks her feet, and bounces off the wall in her first real fit of rage. I've seen tears of sadness---unfortunately, ones I've caused, but these water-works are different. My doll is a one-woman storm of wrath on a path of destruction.

"I can't believe Lupo's men let him get away! You said they were the best!" She lifts a vase over her head, stops to inspect it then places it back on the shelf. There's my Bee. That vase belongs to Tara. She may be furious, but she's not a jerk.

I hold my hands out and urge her to calm down, fully aware anything I say might only piss her off more. "Let me finish, baby. I know you're mad, but he's not lost. He just wasn't where he was supposed to be. The little shit is hiding at his attorney's home, too scared to show his face. But don't worry. Tony Ponti spoke to the judge earlier today, and they've issued a bench warrant for his arrest."

Her brown eyes widen, and her mouth tips into a saucy smirk. "They have? Can they get him there? Now?" She marches into the kitchen and steps onto a tiny ladder to pull two wine glasses from the shelf. Her eyes move back and forth, scanning familiar territory with confusion as her mind spins with renewed thoughts of vengeance. "I've waited this long. I just don't want him to leave the country with my money and make me spend the next twenty years hunting him down. We need to do something, Divo. I can't sit around here and wait for the other shoe to drop."

"He can't leave the country. The judge revoked his passport and alerted customs that he may try to flee the country. Tony said we're just waiting for them to reinstate the earlier will." I uncork a bottle of Cabernet and let it breathe, hoping the news settles her nerves. It doesn't.

"I don't trust him. If he's hiding, he's plotting, and if he's plotting, he'll find a way to screw me over! This won't be the end of it. He didn't do all this to slink away with nothing." She paces, biting her nails and tapping her bare feet on the hardwood floor. "I need to see Hugo." She swipes the glass of Cabernet out of my hand, takes a swig, and darts into the living room.

Hugo? Who the hell is Hugo? My brain freezes on the first taste of Cabernet and locks on that suspicious name. In my daze, I forget to swallow and clutch my throat, choking and gasping for air like an idiot. I spit out what's left in my mouth and chase her upstairs. "Where are you going?"

"I need to change, sweetheart. We need to see Hugo Chamberlain. I should have seen him earlier, but I was too embarrassed." She rushes into her bedroom and bolts into her closet, yanking clothes off hangers and pulling a pair of boots from a shelf.

"Hugo Chamber...lain?" I stutter and follow her into her bedroom. "You said you were kidding! Didn't you say you made him up?" I bark, stunned by her lies and trying to refresh her memory. "Explain yourself, damn it."

Bee looks over her shoulder and flashes a sympathetic smile. "I never said I made him up. I said I was kidding." She jumps into a pair of leggings and unrolls her socks, standing on one leg to slide each one onto her feet. "I just threw out his name because it was the first that came to mind---let it go. He lived next door to me growing up. Well, he still lives next door to my dad's house. But it's more than that. He runs a security tech company and wired our house years ago. Geoffrey may have changed the locks, but I doubt he had the whole system rewired. I've got heirlooms he could sell and paintings he could steal. I bet if I asked Hugo nicely or if Enzo's goons came with us, we might be able to persuade him to let us peek into the cameras of our old security system or maybe break the code." She peels off her tank top and slips into a sweater. For the first time in our relationship, I'm too frazzled to ogle her breasts.

"No, that doesn't make any sense." I cross my arms over my chest and stare down at her impatient expression.

"Sense? What part?" She swipes her watch off the night-stand and buckles it onto her wrist. "We need to leave. Should I call Antonio now or on the way?"

"You don't just pull a name like Hugo Chamberlain out of thin air. Despite my reputation, I'm not an airhead. I studied Freud." I'm hot on her heels, buzzing like a gnat in her ear down two flights of stairs. Am I jealous? Of course, I am. Bee is my world. I've never hidden my psychopathic need to horde her all to myself. Whoever this Hugo character is, she obviously had him on the tip of her brain to just shout him out at her earliest convenience, and frankly, I don't like it. And I'm not so sure I want to pay him a visit.

We reach the bottom of the stairs, and she spins on her heels, smiling innocently as she hands me her coat. She waits for me to hold it open, then slips her arms into the sleeves. I snuggle it onto her shoulders and then slam her into my chest, holding her captive in my arms. "Spill it, little girl."

"You promise you won't get mad?" She looks back and rests her head on her shoulder.

My heart races with rage, but I grit my teeth, produce a fake smile, and nod for her sake. "Don't push your luck."

"He's practically my dad's age, and they were friends, but he looks like a freaking movie star. He was always a sweetheart to me, and I had a huge crush on him growing up. Sorry! It's not like anything ever happened between us. He probably thinks of me as a little girl." She waits for me to answer, but my bug-eyed, lifeless expression gives her little hope for a rational response.

"For heaven's sake, I'm sure I'm not the first girl you ever liked!" She marches out of my arms and heads for the door. "We're going, mister. I need his help, so you better not embarrass me with your crazy-ass ways." She pulls her winter hat over her head and flies through the door.

Once again, I chase after her, growling and shaking my fist in the air like an old man, "You don't know who I did or didn't like. And I swear to God, Bianca, you better behave."

CHAPTER 10
BIANCA

"DIVO BERNARDO TALERICO, I have never been so humiliated in all my life." I storm through the back door of my father's house for the first time in three months and find it deserted. The furniture appears rearranged, my late mother's painting is missing from the mantle over the fireplace, but my father's collection of masterpieces is still in place. It doesn't smell like home anymore. I'll need to air it out to remove the stench of Geoffrey's offensive cigars.

Hugo Chamberlain needed little convincing. He's simmered for months watching Geoffrey Kimble take over my father's house and company and wondered when I'd come around asking for help. Next door, he and Tony are working with one of the city's best hackers, a former employee of Chamberlain Technologies, to raid Geoffrey's personal accounts. He came to town with nothing, and as far as I'm concerned, he'll leave with nothing. I'd rather give his pocket change to panhandlers than let him leave with one red cent of my father's money.

But that's not nearly enough. Enzo Lupo doesn't appreciate untidy endings, and neither do I. He promised to help me, and in lieu of the will, he's paying a personal visit to

Geoffrey's attorney to flush him out of his hiding place. We'll know more in the next hour.

"Humiliated? You're here, aren't you?" Divo zips past me, shoves me against the wall, and holds his gun vertically against his chest. "And how many times did I say let me come in first? How am I supposed to keep you safe if you won't follow directions?" He peers over his shoulders and narrows his gaze to suspicious slits, still fuming over non-existent slights.

I try to wiggle free, but he holds me steady, deliberately pinning me against the wall to prove his point. "Please, wait. I think I hear something."

"You didn't have to pull a gun on him," I whisper and listen for the imaginary noises he claims to hear. "He cooperated from the start. There was no need for violence." I wrestle free and tiptoe into the hall, searching the rooms for any missing items.

"He hesitated, and you know it," Divo fires back, slithering through the hall, still seething over Hugo's resemblance to Superman. I warned him he was attractive.

"He hesitated because you scared the hell out of him." I shake my head with condescension and peek into the kitchen, weaving past his giant frame to pop my head into the dining room and circle back. Where the hell has this man been staying, and how long has he been planning his escape?

Divo groans, "Stop defending your little crush. He's a big boy. And he seemed well acquainted with Tony, which means he's no goody-two-shoes and probably familiar with my line of work." He stuffs his gun into a holster under his shoulder and sticks to me like glue, bumping into my heels and crashing into my face when I change trajectories.

"I'm just saying you went over the top. We can drop it now." I hop to one side, circle past the main entryway, and head upstairs, eager and nervous to see what that rat did with the antiques.

"No, we're not dropping it. You were flirting, and you know it," he growls, catches my waist, and spins me around to face him. "Admit you were flirting. You were giggling so much you sounded like a deranged hyena."

I take offense and boldly deny his accusation. "I was scared. You had a gun in his face...and..." Caught in my web of lies, I spin my wheels and try to weave a believable story of fear mixed with the sudden proximity to my childhood home and the possibility of me ordering Geoffrey's maiming and... "Fine! Maybe I flirted, but it wasn't on purpose. You said yourself he's attractive, and he made me nervous. I felt like a teenager."

Divo's expression twists with the obvious signs of pain. He takes a shaky breath, inhaling through his nostrils as his hazel eyes darken and then twitch. His lips part, then seal shut.

I run my hand down his chest and try to soothe his fractured ego. "I said he's handsome. I never said he's better looking than you."

"I'm going to count to three..." His stern voice makes me jump. I look from side to side, searching my old terrain for hiding places as a mix of panic and naughty thrills make my heart tap dance to an erotic tune. I lift my gaze and stare into his dead eyes. He means business.

"You wouldn't dare," I scream as I flee and try to remember the location of the security cameras.

"One!" Divo paces himself, ambling like a madman in a slasher film, peeling his heavy coat off his sculpted arms as he struts towards my bedroom.

"Leave me alone!" I tease and make enough noise to help him find me. Why do I encourage him? And what's gotten into me?

I used to be a good girl---I'm not kidding. Before Divo, I'd kissed one boy, and we hardly used tongue. Now I'm breaking locks, hacking into bank accounts, encouraging someone to beat my uncle to a pulp, and consorting with mobsters who intimidate attorneys. And if that's not bad enough---now I'm sneaking into a closet, pulling down my leggings, and waiting for my gangster boyfriend to punish me with his cock.

How low can I go?

***

DIVO

I couldn't believe my fucking eyes. No, I could believe them, and that's why I wanted to gouge them out. Hugo's not mine. Bee giggled, batted her lashes, blushed, and fanned her face with her father's will like she was having a hot flash directly in front of me. When I gave her the stink eye, she cooled her jets and then played the innocent, pretending I'd lost my mind. She was right. I had lost my goddamn mind, and I was seconds from having a psychotic breakdown all over Hugo Chamberlain's pretty-boy face.

"Three!" I jiggle the knob and make her sweat. "Do you have something to say for yourself?"

The door cracks open, and a pair of leggings appear. "Sorry, baby. I was out of line."

"Hand over the panties," I demand and hold out my hand.

She places a lacy piece of fabric in my palm, and I stuff it into my pocket. Fearing a nearby camera, I slink into the darkness through a crack and feel my doll's naked tits land in my hands. "Superman, huh?"

"Divo, I was a little girl. You can't hold that against me," her breath rasps as my fingers explore her taut nipples.

"I will hold it against you. You're mine, baby. These are mine." I step closer and trace the swell of her breasts, kneading her supple flesh until the heat of her skin radiates through me, awakening every molecule and heightening my drive to breed my girl---a recent yearning I can't shake from my thoughts. We can finally be together the way we're meant to be together, and I can't wait to drag Bee down the aisle. "Say they're mine."

"They're yours." She melts into my arms and purrs against my lips. I taste her kiss, exploring her mouth with my tongue until I'm unsure where she starts and I end. It doesn't matter anyway. We're one soul fighting to reconnect with the other half. That's the way it's always felt with my doll. She completes me.

"This is mine." I reach between her legs and run my hand through her slit, teasing her swollen clit with my fingers. Her smoldering gaze meets mine, and I lose myself in the deep dark wells of Bianca's brown eyes, the place I've searched for all my life. "I love you, sweetheart. You're about to become one of the wealthiest women in New York, and maybe you..."

"Shut your mouth, Divo!" Bee brings her lips back to mine and crushes her breasts to my chest. I unzip my jeans and unleash the stiff cock seconds from ripping through my zipper.

"You're my man. Do you hear me? You're my man, and I'm your woman," she whimpers into our kiss and tries to climb my thighs. I seal my hungry hands to her luscious ass and help her along.

"You better fucking believe I'm your man. And your man needs to carve his name all over this pussy. Marry me, Bee. I've wanted to ask for so long, doll. Marry me." I shove my cock into her wet pussy and cram it deep, settling her legs around my waist until she's fully impaled.

Her big brown eyes flare with the sudden surprise of being stuffed to the hilt, then hood, fluttering dreamily with the look of lust. She nods and sinks her pearly whites into her bottom lip, sucking her pout into her mouth. "I'll marry you. What would I do without this big cock?" She throws her arms around my neck, shoves her nipples in my face, and bounces on my cock. She gallops and rolls her hips, using her tight pussy to swallow my shaft, once, twice, again and again, leaving me breathless, mind spinning, legs shaking, balls aching, and heart racing with so much love I could carry her naked body straight to city hall now.

"Fuck, I love you, Bee. You're my girl." I hold her against the wall and piston like a diesel engine, thrusting and pummeling into her sweet pussy with a crazed frenzy that sends me to the brink of madness. She's my greatest weakness and the one person who could bring me to my knees, but I never feel more powerful than when I'm in her arms.

"I'm your girl." Her body tightens around me, clamping down as tiny spasms make her tremble through screams. I drag my tongue down the seam of her mouth, devouring her kiss until the divine clench of her climax milks me dry.

I thread my fingers through her hair and kiss every ounce of skin my lips can reach. "Time's gotten away from us, baby. Lupo is probably on his way here with your uncle. Are you ready to kick some ass?"

She quirks one eyebrow and jumps off my hips. "I'm ready."

CHAPTER 11
EPILOGUE-TWO YEARS LATER

DIVO

TWO YEARS AGO, I joined the long line of Talerico men who married a woman far out of his league. Bee became my wife, my queen, and my partner in crime. Of course, she's my silent partner, but the woman behind the man still has a company to run, and Barnes Inc. gives us a face of legitimacy and some hope for the future.

We both agree we want better for our children---when we get around to having them.

Like the men who came before me, I'm happier than a clam at high tide and utterly undeserving of such bliss. Can you believe the nerve I had to approach a woman like Bianca Barnes, sweep her off her feet when I was technically engaged to another woman, hoping and praying I could worm my way out, then still manage to win my doll's hand in marriage? She's a saint.

Fortunately for me, she only has the heart of a saint. That girl walked right into my filthy clutches and allowed me to thoroughly corrupt her. They've been the best two years of my life, and I can't wait for the next sixty.

"Take me to the house on 97th Street, please." I give my instructions to the driver and jump into the backseat. Bianca made me promise to leave work early and head uptown by 4:00. She has a surprise.

The last two years have been a blur, but things are finally settling down. Bianca doesn't like to talk about her Uncle Geoffrey anymore. She's washed her hands of the whole business and wants to put that chapter of her life to rest. But I'll come clean about that weasel. He's lucky he's alive and only walking with a permanent limp.

As expected, his attorneys weren't prepared to hide him once Hugo and Bianca turned off the well to her money. They kicked him to the curb so fast, he left skid marks on the sidewalk. Enzo brought him here and forced him to admit the second will was a forgery. Everyone took turns kicking the shit out of him until he confessed, and then one of our associates broke his legs for good measure.

But it could have been far worse. I've seen guys like him wind up in the East River. Bianca wanted to say she didn't condone violence but couldn't get the words to fully form on her lips. That bastard put her through hell, and she's only human. For the sake of her conscience, I told her it was out of her control and let her keep her hands clean. I didn't say a word about the tiny laugh she couldn't suppress when Enzo kicked her uncle in the nuts.

Anyway, he should count his lucky stars. His connection to Bee saved his life. But his days living in the lap of luxury are over.

And so are the jackasses who helped him.

Bianca's a wealthy woman now. She calls it our money, but I didn't marry my girl for her cash. Her big brown eyes, huge heart, sweet curves, and fine pussy are more than enough for me.

She may have cringed at the sight of Geoff's broken body, but her swift retribution came down like the hand of God. Between her money, Enzo's connections, my men, Antonio's legal prowess, and ultimately a little help from her precious

Hugo Chamberlain, she wiped out every crooked law firm on the Upper East Side. They erased bank accounts, ruined credit reports, made law degrees disappear, revoked licenses, and nullified pre-nuptial agreements. And best of all, those assholes had so many enemies, they have no idea who to blame.

It was a criminal masterpiece and the talk of Manhattan for over a year.

"Sweetheart, I'm home. Bianca?" I stride into the house and march upstairs to search for my doll. "Are you home?"

"Yes." I hear a tiny squeak coming from the closet.

I loosen my tie and slip it over my head. "Why are you in there?"

The door creaks open, and a balled fist appears. She unfurls it and produces a tiny black thong.

"Is that for me?" I twirl it on my finger and fling it on the bed. "What else do you have for me?" She giggles sweetly, and my cock stands at attention.

"This." Bee's small hand emerges, holding tightly to a pink and white plastic stick. I blink twice and try to focus on the object in front of my face. It's a pregnancy test. Bee's got a pregnancy test.

"Holy shit, you're pregnant." I swing open the door and find my beautiful, naked wife standing on the other side, nodding with a face full of tears.

"You're going to be a Daddy!" She jumps into my grateful arms and again makes me wonder how the hell I ever made this perfect doll fall in love with me.

"That's right. Now, you'll have to call me Daddy."

"I'm not calling you Daddy on a regular basis. The baby will call you Daddy."

"Don't fight me, Bee. I don't make the rules."

THANKS FOR READING!

. . .

Would you like to read more about Gala and Enzo?
Read Vanished in Manhattan now!
Would you like to read about Tara and Lance
Read Simmering with the Sous Chef now!
Do you want to read more about Hugo Chamberlain?
Look for Touch of Greed- Coming this August!

CRIMINAL DESIRES

Villains do bad things, like lie, and cheat, and steal. But every bad guy has a backstory and every Bonnie needs her Clyde. This May, celebrate the villain.

Eleven sinful couples will burn down the city. When the dust settles, where will you be? **Criminal Desires**, a steamy romance collaboration that'll melt your eReader.

Happily ever after, guaranteed! ♥

Order the entire series here

Good Girls Finish Last by Kelsie Calloway

Where Roses Lay by Ember Davis

The Thief's Lover by Sadie King

Nights In Paradise by Tamrin Banks

A Delicate Proposition by Layne Daniels

A Taste For Revenge by Pippa Lux

Deal With The Devil by Kylie Marcus

Called By The Dark by Demri

Secret Weapon by Matilda Martel

Returning The Favor by Shyla Colt

My Escape by Sammi Starlight

ALSO BY MATILDA MARTEL

Would you like to read more about Gala and Enzo?

Read Vanished in Manhattan now!

Would you like to read about Tara and Lance

Read Simmering with the Sous Chef now!

Do you want to read more about Hugo Chamberlain?

Look for Touch of Greed- Coming this August!

DO YOU LOVE STEAMY AGE GAP ROMANCE?

Those are my favorites.

If you like them as much as me,

you might like these titles:

We'll Always Have Paris

My Second Chance

Vanished in Manhattan

Takeover

Blind Faith

Happenstance

Simmering for the Sous Chef

Off the Market

Blindsided

Get Your Kicks

The Pastor

In Praise of Older Men

My Heart's Desire

Maestro

Gilded Cage

Love Match

Play Right

The Man I Love

Bad Boss

Clever Girl

Chasing Zoe

The Good Girl

My Ward

Do you love Billionaire Romances?
Try these titles:
Takeover

Filthy Rich

Filthy Love

Blindsided

Gilded Cage

Magic Man

Hostile Takeover

There She Goes

Agreeably Arranged

Bad Boy

Do you love Friends to Lovers?
Shut Up & Kiss Me

Unsuitable

Lucky Man

Marry Me

Do you love Mafia Romances?
Check out my BROOKLYN BAD BOYS
Love Interrupted

Love Unleashed

Love Revealed

And

Vanished in Manhattan

Secret Weapon

BAD BOYS TURNED GOOD?

Check out SCOUNDRELS IN LOVE

Bad Professor

Bad Boss

Bad Boy

PHILLY BOYS FIND LOVE IN LOVE BITES

Love Hate

Love Nest

Love Match

And many more - find them HERE

Thanks for reading and I hope you come back again!

STALK THE AUTHOR

Matilda is a Texas girl in love with a Philly boy who loves to write dirty books about two people who trip into love and fumble their way into a Filthy, Funny, Happily Ever After.

I live in Austin, with my husband, two crazy Chihuahuas and an even crazier cat. And I spend most of my day writing dirty romance books about older men who fall in love with younger women and make fools of themselves trying to win their hearts.

If you love Dark Romance, you've come to the wrong place. I don't like dark heroes.

I like my hero to be successful, sweet, suave, sophisticated and kind--- and then I want him to lose all his composure and game when he meets the heroine. I want him to turn into a bumbling idiot when he spots the girl of his dreams and revert to a teenage boy in a man's body trying to win her.

I like my heroines to be witty, intelligent, and unshakeable---who could do just as well without a man—until the hero convinces her otherwise.

I write A LOT OF AGE GAP--because I LOVE AGE GAP ROMANCE. I've got no other excuse for it.

No matter what kind of story it is, my ladies are ADORED, and my endings are always Happily EVER AFTER, not HFN.

To receive a free ebook, join Matilda Martel's newsletter.

Please head to my website to learn what's in the final stages and will be coming out soon!